Love to Jan
from
Pip

STRANGE TALES

This is the author's second publication. The first book being delightful children's verse.

This book of short stories is for the adult reader, as the events depicted are bizarre to say the least. The tales are based on facts collected by the writer over the years; but it is up to the reader to decide the significance of the happenings.

By the same author:
Children's Treasure House of Poetry

STRANGE TALES

Dr Mildred Sproxton,
Ph.D.,(Educ.), B.Mus.

ARTHUR H. STOCKWELL LTD.
Elms Court   Ilfracombe
Devon

ISBN 0 7223 2131-7

Printed in Great Britain by
Arthur H. Stockwell Ltd.
Elms Court   Ilfracombe
Devon

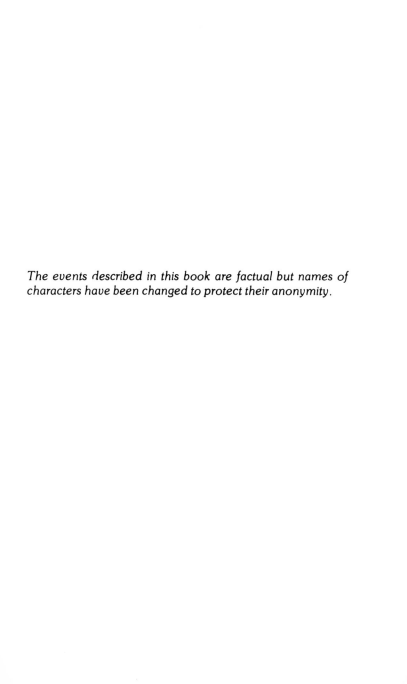

The events described in this book are factual but names of characters have been changed to protect their anonymity.

CONTENTS

FOREWORD

These tales are all based on facts and true incidents which have been collected by the author over a period of some years. There are still many, many events in our experience for which we can offer no rational and satisfactory explanation.

INTRODUCTION

It was this first unusual, strange, and indeed rather eerie occurrence that I am relating that made me decide to record several other odd happenings that have come my way, and that perhaps you might care to hear about.

That particular day in early autumn, there was a feeling of depressing dampness in the air as I made my way towards the wood that was a short cut to Jayne's cottage.

Though the undergrowth seemed more intensely thick than usual and the trees felt almost as though they had moved more closely together since I last went through, I pushed on spurred by the thought that I should see her all the sooner.

The tangled leaves from the overhanging branches brushed my face as I pushed along, and the eerie dampness left irregular mould-laden streaks as I swept them aside with a dank hand. Then — I stopped sharply in utter disbelief — and retraced my steps to the last offending tree and reached upwards to the straggling cascade that I had just moved from my face. It *was* Jayne's perfume! In horror I realised I was right! As I looked upwards the strands of her hair were hanging with the leaf fronds, and her waxen, immobile face, part hidden by the fragrant, moist locks was without life.

Temporarily losing a grip on myself I sped through the rest of the undergrowth, cursing as I did so as the waving foliage struck at my face.

11

Racing towards the cottage and unceremoniously into the kitchen — Thank God! She was there!

"Suddenly I was horribly afraid that you wouldn't come," she cried, rushing at me and holding so tightly that the woody dampness still on my face, fell on her hair, "I felt so incomplete somehow without you that I think I must change my mind about our marriage."

"Then you are saying 'Yes' at last," I cried with unsuppressed joy.

"What do you think?" was her answer.

We walked back together through the wood, and as we went I looked carefully for the face and the perfumed tresses, but no — I did not see anything but the struggling, twisted stems with their weary fronds still mistily clawing at the steamy atmosphere.

DO YOU BELIEVE MARY?

I am of the opinion that though the story-tellers set their tales in the graveyards ready for the appearance of their ghosts, that in truth the spirits are all gone long before even the last 'dust to dust' has been scattered over the coffin.

Animals are well known for their 'sixth sense'. We all have heard of dogs or cats that find their way back to their homes sometimes hundreds of miles away, even if in the first place they were taken away in a vehicle.

An old aunt of mine used to drive a mini, and came to see me every Saturday — arriving at any time of the day that suited her. I always knew in advance however, what time she would be at our door because, though she lived some five miles away my little terrier Tuppy, some quarter of an hour before she actually arrived would run to the window, on to the back of the settee and sit solemnly looking out and waiting for her. We reckoned he made his first move at the exact time that she set off, because sometimes if she were held up by traffic he would wait that little bit longer, and then make his usual run to the door about ten seconds before she turned the last corner.

My point is that I'm sure that sheep, although supposed, I believe, to be among the least intelligent of the four-legged animal kingdom, would never graze happily and comfortably in a churchyard among the tombstones, were there spirits hanging about.

I did hear however, rather a strange tale of a graveyard

13

occurrence which you will probably find of interest.

The Burrows family had been interred in the St. John's Churchyard in Seton village in North Yorkshire for four generations. Great grandpa Joseph, grandpa Thomas, father Peter, and little Johnnie Burrows were all there side by side, their respective tombstones varying from Joseph's Victorian monstrosity of oversized angels down to the little cupid that guarded the grave of little Johnnie.

My friend Mary tells me that she remembers the date well. It was January 21st, and a bitterly cold, snowy day. It was about six o'clock in the evening, and the only light therefore came from the stained glass windows of the church where the organist was busy practising ready for the service the following day.

Her quickest way home was through the churchyard. She had been through many times before, so it was quite frightening in fact, terrifying, for as she hurried past the Burrows' graves an unexpected flash of light from the church windows spread across them, and she saw (and she insists she really DID see) a figure standing on each of the four Burrows' graves. They were holding hands across the narrow strip of land between each of them — a very old man on the first and a small child on the fourth. They looked happy, indeed almost ecstatic as they stretched ethereally sideways fingers touching fingers.

Mary was rooted to the ground for several seconds until the spell was broken by the appearance of the moon — and as she looked the figures disappeared in its lengthening beams.

When she told others of what she had seen some said it must have been the reflection cast by the figures on the stained glass windows of the church, some said that it must have been the sheep seeking protection from the wind behind the stone erections, and others that the eccentric widow woman Dame Walley had hung her washing there for the night but....

I know Mary and I believe her, that she really did see

them and that it was a family reunion, because the next day in clear daylight, looking at the worn carvings I saw for the first time that the date of death of all the four Burrows family was the same in each case. It was the 21st January!

THE CRUISE OF A LIFETIME

I love the sea. It always seems to have a message for me. This time it was saying, 'Come aboard. This will be the best cruise you could have. I will be ever tranquil calm and draw all the sun's rays.' Too imaginative I suppose, my husband is always accusing me of that failing.

However, he agreed to my digging into our hard-earned savings to have, just for this one time an unforgettable trip on the *Queen Elizabeth,* and it was with great joy and enthusiasm that I embarked on this holiday cruise of a lifetime.

We were to sail to New York, starting from Southampton. What a wonderful feeling it was actually to be a passenger on this great liner, and not simply a rather envious spectator watching its departure from the dock.

So, we set sail towards Cherbourg on a clear calm sea in the early evening. Having unpacked my belongings and made my cabin look reasonably tidy I decided to take a stroll on deck whilst it was fairly quiet, it being the time for the evening meal, and both hunger and curiosity about the reports of the wonderful cuisine had drawn most people into the dining-room.

Leaning over the handrail I gazed down into the placid waters of my friend, the sea. Which came first I just do not know, but a sudden squall as unexpected as it was fierce made me grasp the bar with all my strength, and I saw a passenger making similar efforts as he came towards me. Then — to my horror, one exceptionally vicious wind lash

16

hit him and seemed to lift him completely off his feet into the air, and he was tossed over the side like a bundle of rags. The splash as he hit the water appeared to act like a curtain on the sudden freakish weather, and immediate lull and calm reigned as it had when I first went on deck.

Panic stricken I struggled with a hanging lifebelt but was unable to release it so, as one possessed I raced into the dining-room and gasped out my fears to the captain who quickly mustered a posse of men to search for the drowning man.

How long they spent I really don't know. I suppose it must have been several hours in a fruitless search until finally the captain issued instructions that everybody be called together for a complete roll call. He gave me rather a strange look as he came to the end of the extremely lengthy list of names. No one was missing apparently. As an added precaution he went through the arduous task once again but still found all present and correct.

For the next twenty-four hours everybody eyed me in rather a sideways manner as if at someone just a little off normal, a bit unreliable, possibly a hysterical woman who would use any means to draw attention to herself, and certainly a person to be avoided for fear of being tainted. I, in my turn took the hint and spent the second day in my cabin wondering if I really had suffered some sort of hallucination, and that perhaps the young man had existed only in my imagination prompted by the excitement of having in prospect this wonderful trip.

Later in the evening I peered nervously out, still rather reluctant to meet any of those whom I appeared to have so grossly inconvenienced. It was peaceful and quiet. I reckoned we would be about half-way across the Atlantic by now so I ventured again on to the upper deck as on my very first night. Oh! No! Not the same squall again! It certainly was. The wind lashed the rain across the deck and I clung fearfully to the rail. It was almost incredible what happened next. The same young man materialised on the deck. It was almost with relief that I realised I must have imagined the first meeting for here he was, alive and well. That sensation lasted only a very short time. With a final shriek the gale seized him, lifted him high in the air and tossed him over the rail. As he struck the water the rising spume coincided with a complete cessation of the wind, and the violence of the weather decreased as rapidly as it had begun.

Should I go for help again? My mind went hither and thither before making the final decision not to make a fool of myself once more, so I did nothing but returned to my cabin where a disturbed and turbulent sleep awaited me.

The following morning there was a polite tap on the door. "Everybody on the first deck please madam. Just a precautionary check on the passengers. One young man has been reported missing," the steward informed me.

My heart sank as the roll call was repeated, once, twice and even a third time. He really had disappeared.

Was it the young man I had seen thrown overboard in the gale? Could I have risked ridicule and saved him by calling for help?

What would you have done?

That was a very exciting cruise on the *Queen Elizabeth* but it was an experience which, on the whole I don't wish to be repeated!

HOW ODD!

John Evans was just an ordinary chap — well balanced, with an ordinary, humdrum, regular everyday life. Up at 7.30 a.m. and off to work at 8.30 a.m. at the factory where he acted as foreman in the machine room of a printing works — sandwich lunch at the bench with a mug of strong tea, leave at 5 p.m., and off home on the bus.

There was nothing about him to suggest in any way that he was over-imaginative or had any sort of leaning towards the supernatural. A single pint in the 'local' was the extent of any drink he ever took, so why should it happen to John? But it did.

His favourite pastime at the weekends was fishing. There was a clear, gently flowing stretch of water that ran alongside the canal at Rodley, only a fifteen minute walk away from his home. Off he would go on a Saturday morning — with all the 'gear' and an optimistically capacious bag to receive an equally optimistic 'catch', after he had relieved it of the usual sandwiches and flask of highly sweetened tea.

So, on a date that he now remembers well — Saturday, 1st February 1986 — he made his way to his favourite river bank, prepared and threw out his line and settled down to await the attention of the piscatorial world just below his gaze.

He must have dozed in the peace and tranquillity around him for he wakened with a start, looked at his watch and realised that he had been sitting there some half-hour. He reeled in the line, thinking that a prospective catch had made a tug and disturbed him — but, nothing there — his original bait still hung temptingly. Recasting the line he reached for his bag and dug in for the anticipated lunch. That hand he withdrew rapidly as he immediately realised he had contacted something wet and slippery. He peered in the bag — it was full, yes literally brimming with newly-caught fish — more than he had captured in a couple of years! Feeling gingerly among what proved to be a mass of flatties, codling, bream, etc., he felt about for the bottom of the bag for his lunch. There was nothing — nothing but the torn remains of the paper wrappings, and at the very base of all was his flask — quite empty — not even a single drop of tea.

John got up, threw the now heavy, fish-laden bag over his shoulder like a sack and set off for home where he replenished the inner man and made a very strong mug of tea.

He never did understand that extraordinary happening on that extraordinary Saturday!

One thing is quite certain — with all that beautiful fresh fish he came to realise how many friends he had!

REFLECTIONS

We all know the story of the Queen in *Snow White* and her extraordinary mirror, mirror on the wall, but here is a tale of an even stranger one that seemed not to reflect truthful answers as in the fairy story, but replies that the questioner *wanted* to hear. A real 'Yes man' mirror if ever there was one.

I was about thirteen at the time and just beginning to take an interest in my appearance, not too much mind you as being rather a sensitive lad I could not have stood the 'ribbing' of my pals, but just enough to look in the glass sometimes and feel my chin hopefully for an incipient beard.

The school I attended was a mixed one, and up to that moment I had always taken girls for granted — just another pupil — but it seemed to come upon me suddenly that day that Jessie Grey, who was in my class, was gazing at me thoughtfully. At first I looked away quickly but something made me turn towards her again. She was still looking, so this time I stared back and became aware for the first time of her lovely light skin, fair curling locks and sweet mouth, and the hair on the back of my neck seemed to rise, and I wondered if she saw me as I saw her.

Hence the beginning of my, at first, occasional and then regular look at myself in the little square wood-framed mirror in the kitchen.

It was on one such day (it is now so long ago that I cannot remember the exact date), that as I stared intently into the glass thinking that perhaps I wasn't too bad a looking bloke and that Jessie could not find anyone more handsome than I, that the mirror first spoke. It was a whiny, smarmy sound which issued from the wooden frame in its top, right-hand corner. "Very nice Pip — very, very nice."

Surprised but flattered, from then on I looked daily at my reflection, and my own self-satisfied opinion of my features grew with each unctuous confirmation from the mirror. "Very fine, yes very fine, very attractive indeed" it would say.

Meanwhile my distant gaze at Jessie had developed into assignations behind the shed in the school cricket field. Like almost all romances, the looking and the hand holding had to develop, and it was then that my difficulties appeared. Both Jessie and I had loved our mutual admiration until one day, taking my courage in both hands I pulled her towards me rather roughly and tried to kiss her. Amazed and somewhat annoyed at the resistance that I met, and not believing it possible that my charms were being repulsed, I continued to force her forward.

Suddenly without warning she broke free, hitting me smartly across the cheek with her school satchel. "Don't you ever do that again!" she yelled, "and take your ugly face back home." I opened my mouth to protest but she broke in, "Yes, ugly, you are really the most revolting boy in the class."

Amazed and hurt I went slowly home. With pricked pride I entered the kitchen and sought consolation in the little mirror. "Am I ugly, am I?" I said pitifully.

Of course, agreeing with me as usual the mirror replied, "Yes, indeed you are!" With that my reflection in the glass produced a hideous grin, and its mouth spread rapidly from east to west bringing in its wake a long, deep, ugly horizontal crack in its surface.

As I grew older that break in the little kitchen mirror was a frequent and salutary warning to me whenever I, as my mother would put it, became 'too big for my boots!'

THE SPIRIT IS WILLING BUT.....

I, like many people can see that the theory of reincarnation seems a sound, practical solution to the belief in the resurrection of the spirit, but it wasn't until last year that it became more than just a theory in my eyes.

It was just a normal day — not even in any way extreme weatherwise. It was not a dimly-lit alley-way, nor was it misty under dripping trees or any venue or atmosphere that would suggest mystery of any sort or in any way.

I was a teacher and had taken my form on a history excursion from Leeds to York, to look at the museum and the realistic Victorian street with its truly lifelike models of the period. There was a fine reproduction of the old horse drawn fire-engine with its great hand rung warning bell, and along the cobbled road shops of the 1850s. The children were especially drawn to the exhibition of dental equipment once used, the huge, iron pliers that had been wielded to draw teeth causing oohs and ahs from them all.

A guide approached us and led us to a 'Police Station' explaining something of Victorian law and the real hardships of the prisons in those days. The deprivation of the inmates, the languishing in jail in filthy conditions of men, women and children long before any suggestion of a trial, and the bribing of warders to obtain food of the most basic kind. He made special mention of the 'debtors' who were thrown there and frequently died there as they were unable to make reparation whilst still incarcerated.

He opened the door of a cell and a truly musty smell

23

emerged. I felt sure I could sense the presence of a cowering, terrified human being there, but it was quite empty. The children crowded round daring each other to go in, but to my surprise the guide went in to the little place, closed the door from the inside and after turning the key leaned on the back wall as if exhausted. I gazed at him, puzzled at this rather extraordinary behaviour, and as I watched I know I saw him literally shrivel before my eyes as if a corrosive liquid had been poured over him, first the clothes then his whole structure seemed to disappear into the rough, damp stone wall behind him. I stared, and stared again. There was a completely empty cell.

Hurrying away to keep an eye on my charges who were scattering to have a closer look at the shops, I was approached by a uniformed attendant who astounded me by suggesting that he would act as our guide.

"Thank you" I told him, "but we already have had a guide." I hesitated a little before adding, "I think."

He gave me a peculiar look as he said, "There is no other guide. I am the sole one here."

With a mumbled apology and a last rather furtive look in the direction of the prison cell, I hastily gathered my charges together and we made our way across to the Railway Museum.

ROSES

Some young friends of mine told me of a rather curious experience their parents had in early married life which seemed to have no rational explanation. What do you think about it?

Pat and Beryl had bought their first house in what had once been a rather elegant Victorian terrace, but now as they entered for the first time after all the usual purchasing formalities had been completed it really looked rather sad and forlorn.

Pat had come prepared to attack the cracked plaster of the kitchen, so quickly donning overalls he set to work to remove the wall surface of the old room.

Meanwhile Beryl had put six-week-old baby Joy's carry-cot on the old kitchen table, and filling a vase with water she put in it some lovely bright red roses which she felt would give some cheer to the place, and carried them to the adjoining sitting-room.

Here the fireplace was, or had been, a beauty. The mantelpiece and surround were of pure white marble, and the old hearth had a foot high elaborate wrought iron fender to contain safely any stray coals that might have escaped from the vast grate.

A sound from the carry-cot broke in sharply on her dreamy contemplation, and she quickly placed the vase on the broad mantelpiece and returned to the kitchen.

It was lovely to feel that this was to be theirs, just theirs, a place of their own at last — somewhere they could be together as a little family — somewhere they could make into a real home, furnished and decorated to their own taste. Having lived for the first two years of their marriage with Beryl's parents whilst saving for that all important 'deposit' for a house they felt somehow that at last their real marriage was just beginning.

Beryl fed little Joy, 'winded' her and put her down again to sleep. The tranquillity and sense of perfection were suddenly interrupted by a sharp crash followed by the sound of breaking glass. The couple both ran to the sitting-room. Red roses were scattered widely over the room and shattered slivers of glass lay on the floor against the wall opposite to the fireplace, which was some fifteen feet away!

They both stood aghast for a full ten seconds. Later neither was able to offer a rational explanation for the occurrence. Had Beryl in her hurry on hearing the baby perhaps not put the vase far enough on the mantelpiece and it had overbalanced, she knew it would have fallen straight down into the hearth and been mainly contained within the high wrought iron surround. It seemed as if it had been thrown, and with considerable force from one side of the room to the other!

Gradually Pat, Beryl and baby Joy settled in their new house and lived very happily there. It turned from a sad empty shell into a home, and as the years went by Joy grew up, went to school, married and even had her own little family.

Grandparents Pat and Beryl still live at No. 23, Welling Road, Hull, peacefully and without any major incident or catastrophe ever, happily, coming their way but I'm sure you will understand why, in all those years something — I don't know what — prevented Beryl or Pat from ever putting red roses, or any flowers for that matter, on the sitting-room mantelpiece.

There must be another story behind that somewhere. Don't you think so?

SUSIE

I always rather 'pooh-poohed' the suggestion that the feline fraternity had something supernatural about them, but suppose that now we have had to accept that witches really do exist and live among us, we should also admit that the cat, particularly the black one usually associated with witches and warlocks, has established a credence in the world of the strange and the uncanny.

As an animal lover I am well aware that people who feel similarly tend to over eulogize about their pets' reactions and responses to us as humans, and being a practical soul take most of these tales with a 'pinch of salt'. That is until the arrival of Susie as we later called her. She was half-grown and almost completely white, and when cleaned up, long and fluffy haired. The only other colour she sported was a black tail which always stood erect like that of an Airedale at a Cruft's Show. This, together with a black dab on an otherwise white head gave her rather an odd and even eerie appearance.

We had just had our beloved St. Bernard put to sleep because of a terminal growth, and like many other animal owners we said, "Never again — no more pets — the emotional aspect of losing one is just too much." So much for that resolution however. During the recent bad winter when the snow fell almost constantly for days and nights on end, this little bedraggled creature appeared from under our hut where she had apparently been sheltering and sleeping for some considerable time. Where she came from we didn't know. Later we came to the conclusion that like Topsy she had 'just growed'. No neighbours had ever seen her before, and nobody claimed her. Having fed her in the garden hut and given her a box lined with carpet for sleeping, you will know of course what was the next logical step in her biography. Yes, she was in the kitchen with a litter tray for nights and comfy cat basket for days. So went our resolution of 'no more pets'.

So far however nothing exceptional happened. She was spayed, and as the months went by she grew into a fine physical Madame Puss.

I think she would be about twelve months old when the first incident occurred. Her real age of course we never knew.

Like most cats she loved to climb but unlike her fellows she never seemed to fear the descent however steep or breath-taking it appeared to us.

On the first occasion we were in the garden and saw her sitting, apparently quite comfortably on the house roof, and when we tried to persuade her to join us on terra firma, with a disdainful swish of the vertical, black brush of a tail she, like Hunt and Hilary went on right to the top. Not content with that, as if well experienced on the tight-rope she stepped daintily along the ridge tiles to the chimney stack and — DISAPPEARED DOWN THE POT!

Consternation was followed by action, and whilst my husband ran for a ladder I rushed into the house just in time to see Susie emerging from the fireplace, quite unruffled and SPOTLESSLY CLEAN — not a spot of soot on that white, fluffy coat, and to cap it all she looked at me disdainfully, strutted outside and proceeded to climb the ladder behind my husband. Not only that but she then joined him in peering down the chimney with curiosity before he realised her presence! I will not record what he said!

There is no rational explanation of this I *saw* her go down and I *saw* her emerge!

Have you any suggestions?

Susie's attitude to other cats was extraordinary. There were several local toms who used our garden as their 'stomping' ground, and they on occasions met and as was their wont had squawking contests for various reasons such as romantic assignations etc., but Susie would step among them as peacemaking referee, and it was the eeriest sight to see her sitting solemnly on the old tree stump — head held high — whiskers uplifted and with several minion toms quietly listening, I'm sure for a lecture on feline manners and etiquette. No howling, no mewing, nothing to do with their desire for a partner, they would sit as if hypnotised by Susie. It was like an entranced audience, respectful and trembling with joy at an audience with the queen.

This happened more than once, and we sometimes used to say that she called the local cats to a solemn meeting over which she presided with regal aplomb.

I came to the conclusion that the big, grey fellow was her consort for they strolled together many times through the orchard and round the gooseberry bushes as if in solemn conclave about the sins of the young.

One thing is certain that as the years go by and Susie herself grows in wisdom there will be many more 'tails' to tell of this unusual animal. She has certainly altered my one-time sceptical views on reincarnation. I am convinced that she was here in years past as Prime Minister or President at the very least.

We await the next incident with interest.

THREE WEEKS LATER!

Almost before I had time to turn round after recording my previous tale you will see from the title our interest was again captivated.

My husband thinking that as my writing was finished for a time resumed what had formerly been his habit of a daily 'tickling of the ivories'. He was playing the marching common time item from Handel's 'Scipio' with his usual strong emphasis of the beat. Busy in the kitchen I listened for a minute or two and wondered why on earth he had put on the metronome with its clear, firm tick-tock, tick-tock, beat by beat. Curiously putting my head round the lounge door I was surprised to see there was no metronome, so I withdrew hastily. The heavy tick-tock continued, and as thoughts of all kinds of possibilities from the death-watch beetle to dry rot in the floor-boards, ran through my mind I began to tour the house to try to solve the mystery.

The reason for the emphasised beat was clear as soon as I entered the bathroom! The bath plug was swinging from one side of the bath to the other and there, sitting over the plug hole was Susie — paw raised as a tennis racquet, batting the offending article rhythmically back and forth IN TIME TO THE SCIPIO MARCH!

It was unbelievable — particularly when the tune below changed to a Chopin waltz and the plug was neatly batted in the new three time by Susie's paw immediately and without hesitation.

I've changed my mind about the former Prime Minister or President. Perhaps after all she was once Sir Henry Wood. Who knows?

SUSIE AGAIN

Not many weeks ago we were in the garden and heard the warning cry of a female blackbird. We recognised the sound as it was quite familiar to us to hear her when an enemy was about. Not that she regarded us as unfriendly but her call to her young indicated the presence of a member of the four-legged variety. The reason for her concern was clear. An inquisitive member of her young family (had it been a child I suppose we should have entitled it hyperactive) had taken an experimental flight from the nest, and was hopping about innocently on the grass quite unaware of the danger mama was trying to point out.

As it is always best to leave a bird in these circumstances and let the mother retrieve the lost one, I simply watched to await the outcome till, to my horror I saw a bundle of white fur move slowly across the lawn towards the scene. Horrified I raced to intercept what I thought might be a massacre but stopped in amazement to see Susie sitting solemnly next to the baby bird, and seemingly using some strange fascination over it so that it ceased its perambulations and stood perfectly still. Then with a warning wave of an admonishing paw as if to say "Just you stay there till your mother comes," my unusual puss joined me, black, feathery tail waving as if in satisfaction at another job well done.

As we went inside together I noted from the corner of my eye Mrs Blackbird fly down and collect her recalcitrant child.

Do you think I should provide Susie with a clerical collar? She certainly loves a morning drink of coffee and I have yet to meet a 'man of the cloth' who has refused one.

WANT A LIFT?

She was tired, her legs ached and it was all she could do to drag the battered shopping trolley into the already open lift. However seventy-six-year-old Mrs Lowe managed it, sank back thankfully and leaned against the lift wall in sheer exhaustion.

It was no picnic, first having been moved from her cosy little terraced house in a 'slum' street in Leeds where neighbours were always within call and shopping was easy. Now she felt not only marooned in her fifth floor flat in this huge, impersonal block in which each eyed the other with suspicion, (and often with just cause may I add) but — afraid, isolated and unwanted. A situation oft repeated in these so-called enlightened days. How many of these elderly, lonely folk were similarly placed, and how many would have exchanged their acquired 'mod cons' for the old friendliness and sense of security, in spite of the cold water tap and the outside toilet?

Mrs Lowe pulled her tired back from the wall, hand outstretched towards the lift panel button for Number Five floor when she was roughly pushed back again by a large, dirty hand, and she bumped her head unpleasantly. The owner of the offending appendage even then did not release her but continued to press hard against her chest, harder, then harder till she felt that each breath was to be her last.

"Where's your purse missis? Give us it quick!" he spoke jerkily. Then addressing a companion who was now leaning on the still open, lift gate he went on, "Keep them doors back till I've got it!"

Poor Mrs Lowe! She managed to gasp out that her purse was in her right-hand pocket, and for a blessed six seconds the heavy hand was taken from her chest as its owner began to tear at her pockets. This temporary relief was followed by a fearful panic when she remembered how small was the amount of money that remained after her shopping expenditure, and what would be the reaction to its discovery by the cruel thug.

Suddenly without any warning there was a movement of the lift. The lounging accomplice had to jump for his life as the gates closed, and as he had been precariously balanced on one foot which was outside the cage he half fell and half rolled into the entrance hall, the gates closed and the lift moved upwards.

Meantime inside the lift Mrs Lowe's assailant was more afraid than she was. He dashed at the wall panel pressing frantically at each floor button, first Floor One but on they went, then Floor Two, still on they went, now Number Three button, still no stop, Number Four — ever upwards *but* as Number Five was approached there was a surprising slowing down. Gently the lift drew to the fifth floor, the doors opened invitingly and our hero dashed out *straight into the arms of two policemen!*

Whilst one hung firmly on to his captive the taller constable put an arm across the pensioner's shoulders, "Come on love," he said, "have you your key? Don't worry. I'll see you safely in."

Still shaking but relieved Mrs Lowe entered her flat, closed the door and made for the kettle and the teapot.

Some little time later as she was checking her shopping she found her purse inside the bag of potatoes. Of course! She remembered slipping it down there for safety.

A knock on the door restarted the former fluttering of her heart, but the familiar voice which she recognised as that of the taller policeman called, "May we come in please?" calmed her fears and he and his colleagues came inside.

C

It seemed that one of their station mates had been following our two villains, thinking they had been acting suspiciously round the entrance to the flats, and on hearing the clang of the lift gates and seeing the rolling fall of our friend he had radioed for help as he hung on to suspect number two.

We can explain how a panda car by chance *could* have been within yards when the call was received, and how with extreme athleticism they *could* have reached the fifth floor as the lift came to a halt, *but* can *you* or anybody for that matter find a reason *why* the lift started to move at so opportune a moment, and especially *why* it stopped only at the fifth floor?

It was odd. It was all very strange. Don't you agree?

THE EBONY STICK

The silver neckband glinted below the firm, bone handle of my late grandfather's walking-stick. It had stood in the old, greenish floral pot stand for as long as I could remember. Its firm, hard ebony body seemed to symbolise generations past. Fine, upstanding, supportive and sometimes punitive, I remember as a child, it represented the reliability and strength of an age now gone.

I was sitting in the hall waiting for a rather important phone call, and being in my late seventies, rather than listening for a distant ring and making a mad dash before the signal ceased which I now find hard to do, I had settled myself comfortably enough on the telephone seat to save any such inconvenience. (One gets very economical in the use of one's energy as old age creeps on.)

I was simply gazing at the old stick and I suppose, as it was rather a warm day, dozing just a little when it moved. It definitely moved — no doubt about that. At first that did not seem very unusual as many articles in any house often have a habit of slight self-adjustment, perhaps due to vibrations or even undue noise, but when it began to rise completely out of its holder and started first to walk and then to swing gaily as if in the grip of an invisible force, my eyes opened wider. It reached the door. Yes — you're right! It was a silent 'Open Sesame' and off it went down the garden path — Up, Down, Ground, Up, Down, Ground as if grandfather were there again and in his twenties making all the happy, jaunty trips of the 1870s, his stiff collar very white, his straw 'benji' at a provocative angle.

What was I to do? Should I follow and try to bring back the recalcitrant cane? The ringing of the phone decided the issue for me. I had to lift the receiver. As I expected it was my elderly sister from Dundee.

"I hope you don't mind Pip but couldn't talk to you before as my grandson John was with me, but I'll come straight to the point now," Madge added, "have you still got grandfather's old walking-stick? Would you hate to part with it very much? It would be just the ideal cane for John. They are quite fashionable again for young men. Do you think you could let him have it? I'm sure it's of no use to you having no children of your own."

There was a rustling sound by the still open door and a flash of silver as if something or somebody was listening very intently.

Feeling perhaps rather mean I heard myself say, "No I'm sorry Madge — its home is here. It lives here. It will always live here."

The phone was put down very heavily at the other end, and I turned round at a murmur like a sigh of contentment from the direction of the entrance. Why I didn't feel surprised at seeing grandpa's stick nestling comfortably in its old place I just don't know.

THE MISSING LINK

Can you think of anything more mundane for the subject of a tale than — A STRING OF SAUSAGES! But this is another true story so I will relate it exactly as it happened.

A sudden desire for an appetising meal of grilled tomatoes, sausages, and bacon, garnished with mushrooms started the ball rolling. Hotplate at the ready, ingredients lined up — all correct — oh no! The sausages were not there!

A hasty re-examination of the freezer revealed that like a great many foods in a family, particularly one with teenage sons, the sausages were absent without leave.

Prompted partly by greed and partly by determination, I grabbed a shopping bag, flung on an anorak, hastily locked the door and off I flew to the village butcher's. Almost champing at the bit at the one customer being served, who could not make up his mind which was the better value of two joints both the same price, both being lamb but the smaller being fillet and the larger a bony piece of shoulder.

Hurriedly I grabbed a string of some dozen porky, pink sausages from the shelf. "How much?" I gasped and banged the requested ninety-two pence on the counter, "Never mind wrapping it."

I was panting as I seized the link in a firm grip and started to push it a piece at a time into my shopper as I ran down the street. However a shaggy mongrel dog had other ideas, and dropping what looked like a piece of cord he fixed his teeth firmly into the last three meaty parts and tugged and tugged. It was an uneven battle. In no time at all he had extracted the whole of the link and I had neither the heart nor the breath to give chase.

As I turned slowly something bright on the pavement caught the sun, and there was a glint from the thief's discarded 'string' as it lay on the ground. Stopping to look more closely I realised that this was something more than some pup's plaything. It certainly was a string, but of what looked like shiny glass beads. Picking it up I popped it into my pocket and made my way home, my enthusiasm for a grill somewhat dampened by now.

My husband seemed not to notice the incompleteness of his meal and wiped his mouth with evident satisfaction after eating, so apparently all was well. But was it? No sooner had we settled down to listen to the TV news than the doorbell rang. The answered ring revealed a constable and a sergeant of the police solemnly holding up a rather battered looking string of sausages. The faces of both men showed that their efforts to control suppressed laughter had not been entirely successful.

"Are these yours madam?" the sergeant asked.

I hesitated before saying, "Well — probably" for positive identification was difficult, especially as there were clear indentations of teeth marks but whether man or beast it was hard to decide. It had a very 'stringy' look — ah 'string' yes! I suddenly remembered the glass beads that had had that appearance. "Just a minute sergeant, I think you had better have these. The dog dropped them this morning," I said as I took the necklace from my pocket, "I had almost forgotten them."

So the strange exchange was made, ornamental link for edible one, and the policemen went back to the station to enter my find in the Lost Property Book.

You will want to know the sequence to this story and I won't hold you in suspense any longer.

No, the necklace was not anybody's missing diamonds.

They were just what they appeared to be. They were ordinary glass beads, not even crystal. Disappointed? I expect you are, but I was not because several days later a little old lady stood timidly on my doorstep. She looked so tired I asked her in for a chat and a cup of tea. She had come to thank me for finding the glass beads. They were all she had, she said, to remind her of her teenage daughter, an only child who had been drowned in a boating accident on Lake Windermere some forty years previously. Now a widow with no family, these bits of glass were indeed precious.

You will probably have guessed that this cup of tea was not the only one we shared but it was the first of many. She even was encouraged by me to bring along her only companion, Scruffy the hairy kleptomaniac who first brought us together.

Eventually Mrs Mayer, his mistress, became our adopted grandmother and thus a third link was made.

A GLIMPSE OF HEAVEN

I remember as a child some seventy years ago how I loved to play in the garden. One corner held a particular attraction for me for in it standing high with age, its twisted branches thrown out like the gnarled arms of a Methuselah, was the old apple tree, and from one of its firmer limbs hung an old length of clothes-line, its many knots indicating the varying sizes of the many youngsters who had climbed upon it.

It was my favourite pastime to sit there dreaming as lone children do.

I was similarly occupied one day as I began to swing — back and forth, back and forth, travelling in an imaginary world all my own. The regular movement first one way then another had a sort of hypnotic effect on my mind and body. The day was warm. It was June and the flowers showed their glorious multicoloured beauty and form against the variegated greens of the background of bushes and trees. There was a slight mist in the air which shrouded the wakening butterflies. It formed a gossamer veil that made me feel that perhaps I could draw it aside to reveal a new and wondrous secret. Surely its delicate shimmering shrouded a mystery.

My legs firmly stretched forward, hands gripping the old rope I began to swing outwards and inwards, outwards and inwards — rising with each push of the toes — higher and yet higher till it appeared that the fragile mist was pierced and I had arrived on a new magic land. This was the heaven I had always anticipated. What a truly wonderful place! The grass was greener than one had thought possible, the flowers more luscious than I had ever seen, and above them all floated not fairies as I had hoped but angels, their robes of silken glory swirling midst white feathery wings.

They stretched out long graceful arms as if beckoning me but I could not move as a strong fierce wind forced a path between us.

I remember nothing more of that land except to try to tell my mother what I had seen when I wakened in bed to find my left leg in a plaster cast and my right arm and head covered in bandages.

According to my parents I had fallen from the swing, and that in spite of repeated warnings from them I had swung too high, falling out and was nearly killed.

Do you think that glorious land was a flash of heaven, and that at the last minute they decided there was not room for me just yet?

Looking back that is what I believe.

THE MAGIC CIRCLE?

It was only recently that I read in my local newspaper of this very odd occurrence which I know will be of interest to you.

It was harvest time — still is for that matter — and the corn was at its most golden, standing straight, firm and full for the sunshine and light rain had shown the kindlier side of nature this time.

The farm was fairly large, consisting of some two hundred acres in all, mostly used for crops although the farmer had some three dozen cows for dairy produce.

You will note I have not named the actual place as already the report in the newspaper had attracted much unwelcome publicity, and I do not wish to exacerbate the situation which has already resulted in sightseers trampling down crops and leaving open farm gates. The public can be thoughtless in many ways when they visit the countryside. Whilst their own suburban patches are absolutely sacrosanct they seem to think that different rules apply to a farmer's property. What moves them — interest perhaps to put it kindly and mildly, curiosity or sheer envy I just do not know. However — to the tale in hand.

The morning that harvesting of the corn was to begin, it was 5.30 a.m. and the farmer went out to wait for his labourers. He employed one man full time and had two part time hands in addition. As he stood gazing at the first golden field and I suppose, possibly as many of us would, reckoning on its value in monetary terms, he suddenly noted what appeared to be a large depression in the centre of the field. He moved closer and stood on the gate to guage

better what he now realised was something rather odd.
There was what looked like a circle of flattened corn some
forty-two feet in diameter that he knew could not be lifted by
the harvester, for although it was not destroyed it was lying
quite horizontally on the ground as if taking a long sleep.
What puzzled him most was the perfection of the circle's
shape. It was as if some giant flying saucer had soothed the
contents of the ring before landing gently on it. A variety of
thoughts came to mind but none offered a satisfactory
explanation for there had been little wind and no sound of
disturbance during the previous night.

The labourers arrived and the harvesting began, one man
having to hand scythe in the flattened circle, a harder task
than today's farm workers are accustomed to, and
consequently done with much less speed than in these
mechanisation days. The outcome was that only one field
yielded its fruit that day.

The following dawn saw the farmer travelling to his
second cornfield where he was extremely annoyed and
dismayed to find another forty-two feet diameter circle of
flattened wheat occupying it. Not only were they already
behind time, but the worker who had hand scythed the
sleeping ears the previous day had not turned up. His
master later learned that the excessive physical work had
made him unfit for further effort for some time and all this
did not improve the farmer's temper. Determined to find
the cause of the strange phenomenon he and his remaining
two workers took a night 'watch' to find out what or who it
was.

They took turns in staying awake. There was always one
on full alert throughout the hours of darkness but nothing
unusual was spied. The air was calm and silent throughout.
As dawn appeared the worker who had scythed the
flattened wheat the previous day tired and stiff announced
that further effort from him was out of the question, and off
he went home to bed.

The farmer and his one remaining assistant tackled the

third field. Unwillingly they hand scythed the crushed centre.

You will probably have guessed that in spite of continued invigilation nothing untoward was found at night time, and that our poor farmer finished with the fourth field graced with the usual circle and no staff left. This time he could not possibly manage the whole himself so he just cut the standing corn and left the rest — unscythed and in peace.

Can you account for any of this? Particularly the fact that when our farmer went out on the fifth day there in yesterday's field stood a complete and perfect circle of *erect* beautiful corn as if the night's sleep had given refreshment and impetus to new life!

He just stared at the vitalised ears — symmetrically set in the midst of their neighbours' stiff, short, sharp stooks. They looked so proud — almost defiant, certainly triumphant — so much so that I quite understand that neither the farmer nor anyone else would go in and cut them down and they were left proudly standing.

I am wondering what will happen when ploughing time comes! Aren't you?

THE CHIMING CLOCKS

We have two striking clocks known as 'grandfathers', one I believe is valuable. We like to think it is an eighteenth century John Harrison, but are unsure. It strikes the hours and the half-hours, but regretfully to me does not have the lovely Westminster chimes, and the other clock is similar in appearance but is an imitation which also strikes the hours and the half-hours. This second 'grandfather' as far as we know, was made some thirty years ago and bought by my father at that time.

To prevent the drawing-room looking somewhat like a watchmaker's shop, and the inevitable varied and constant ticking which sounded as though one could expect a bomb to explode at any minute, (you see I have fourteen clocks altogether of different periods but only the two 'chimers'), rather than have them on a sound collision course the younger of the two 'grandfathers' was put in the adjoining dining-room.

Though separated by a wall we still heard the double striking which to even an unmusical ear was unpleasant as one sounded middle C and the other D one tone above.

Try as my husband did with the strike mechanisms, alterations of which seemed impossible as of course the strike had to synchronise with the correct time — the combating sounds continued. Eventually he decided to stop winding the newer clock so that we heard only the old master with its mellow, musical C.

Peace reigned for a week but explain this if you are able, for after those seven halcyon days we had just heard the half-hour strike in the drawing-room, when there came what sounded like an echo from the dining-room. Going in to investigate we could find nothing there as far as we could see to account for the sound which we knew had its strike mechanism unwound. As we left we decided that some vibration, its source as yet undiscovered, must have caused that echo but events proved that theory wrong for *it continued to happen!* Yes, every time the Harrison struck its counterpart repeated the sound in the other room. Not only that, but as time went on it grew louder and stronger as if in competition.

We never wound the strike of the younger clock again but it still sounded, firmly and musically every time its predecessor played the hour and the half-hour.

Were the two clocks speaking to each other? Had they decided to be friends down the years? Perhaps the Harrison had come to the conclusion that imitation was the sincerest form of flattery? I suppose we shall never know.

Of one thing I am happy to say, they agreed that middle C was worth repeating!

THE THIRD COACH

John Sutcliffe was very old. He had almost achieved (which always seems to me a very strange way of putting it) his century.

His family — one son Harry aged seventy-six and a spinster daughter Mary who was seventy-four, were not shocked to find their father sleeping peacefully one morning, a sleep from which he would never waken, and were relieved at such a quiet passing, and from the contented expression on his face, a happy one.

They all lived at 'Wayside Croft' a farmhouse attached to their one hundred acres of land, now worked by Harry's only son (another John).

Harry and Mary received the doctor's certificate of death which stated 'heart failure' with the resignation which most of us do, for we laymen rarely care to contest a professional opinion on such matters, though that is not to say that queries do not arise in our minds. However the brother and sister were more than content to accept the doctor's verdict for they had dreaded a record which might have used the word 'senile'. Such titles seem to matter so much more, particularly when we are in that emotional state which comes with the passing of a loved one.

The funeral arrangements were made. The burial was to take place in the grounds of the local church. This was St. Patrick's, a beautiful old building where the inscriptions on the tombstones were a history lesson in themselves. Some dated back as far as the sixteen hundreds, others where the late John was to be interred were of a more recent date. Several of those named had been his friends and contemporaries so he would lie with them, and those left on earth would be happy in such circumstances that their father was in the best place.

Only two coaches were ordered, the family being so small, and the cortège made its way sedately followed with respectful pace by the first car holding Harry, his wife and Mary. The second limousine carried a distant cousin who had arrived much to everyone's surprise for the funeral. She was accompanied by 'young' John and his wife.

I, together with several of the villagers stood, hats doffed reverently as the cortège made its solemn way to St. Patrick's. Pretending not to be inquisitive you can imagine that, may God forgive us, we were making mental notes of the occupants. Our curiosity was well satisfied in this respect till we peered at the third coach (though our heads were slightly bowed in reverence it is surprising what one can see even in that posture). Those within were very, very still — shadowy, dark figures in mourning positions — unrecognisable even had we been rude enough to press our noses to the windows. Must be some distant relatives, was the general consensus in our minds as we followed into the church and waited for the procession of mourners as they passed down the aisle. Now we shall find out who was in the third coach was our unspoken thought. Strange — on they came, as expected, Harry, his wife, Mary, young John and his wife and — nobody else! Where were the mysterious occupants of the third coach?

Nor did it solve anything for us bystanders when, after the burial only *two* coaches stood outside to take the family back to 'Wayside Croft'.

I wasn't alone in seeing that third coach and its occupants. We have had to agree that the whole thing was odd, very odd indeed — especially as Harry and Mary insisted later that there had only been two coaches.

There is a feeling that the grave-diggers had opened a door for old John's spirit-friends who had risen to welcome him and settle him with a friendly welcome into his new environment. At least it seemed to me as I stood watching as the coffin was scattered with God's soil that a door was closing and an abiding peace was to reign.

I am glad of that smooth sensation for it is just twenty years since I was buried here, and with the coming of John a cycle was completed and a restlessness I had experienced since interment disappeared.

Thankfully I sank to perfect rest.

TO BE OR NOT TO BE

Carfield Hotel in lovely Pateley Bridge in my dear county of Yorkshire, once known as Carfield Manor dated back to the sixteen hundreds, and there were many stories of ghosts and spirits appearing there, as there are about any historical building — usually without much foundation except in the imagination of the story-teller. However when my friend Jilly was staying there for the weekend she had an interesting experience which I think worth recording.

The owners of the hotel had had the perspicacity to retain as many of the original features of the house as possible, and there were certain areas of structure like the old oak panelling in the lounge which considering its age was in good condition and which they had retained.

The lounge was very comfortable and inviting, and on the day of my friend's arrival, having travelled north by train for much of the day from her home in Somerset, she was glad to rest there and accept the offer of a much needed cup of tea very gladly.

A young assistant approached and asked if he could take her luggage to her room. As this was being arranged she commented on the beautiful panelling. "It must be at least three centuries old surely," Jilly said, "it looks so mellow and comfortable as if it had grown with the room and the house."

"Yes, I believe that is about its age" said the young man, "and of course we have a ghost. He's supposed to be the spirit of a Royalist supporter who was fleeing from the

Roundheads and hid behind the panel. Unfortunately for him the soldiers came, found him and immediately fastened the panel down securely so that he was never able to get out. I expect the skeleton is still somewhere behind there." He pointed to a spot just behind Jilly's chair, picked up the bags and departed up the lovely, curved stairway.

My friend had listened politely but knowing, as I have already stated that such stories are prevalent, thought no more about it. Leaning back in comfort, the tea having soothed away much of the effect of her journey she was disturbed, first by a rustle and then the feeling of a chill wind in her hair. Turning sharply she saw a long wisp of grey swirling gossamer — first sliding very slowly and then, as this smokelike phenomenon gathered speed it seemed to accelerate through her, and as it whirled before her she could distinguish dimly the outline of a helmet, short leather embroidered jacket, curved body shield above strong, tough knee breeches. Though he was helmeted he still appeared to sweep a be-feathered hat from the air as he stretched out a gauntletted hand in which he held a silver goblet — "Ale stranger, ale or I die of thirst, I beg of you," came the eerie sound from the long misty tongue.

Jilly reached for the cup; but what happened then is difficult for her to recall. She does know that at that moment other guests came noisily into the lounge from the dining-room and her cavalier disappeared more quickly than he had arrived.

"What a stupid thing I am," my friend said to herself as she forced herself into full consciousness, "what a dream!"

One of the guests came forward to introduce herself and make her welcome. Jilly stretched out her hand in friendship...

It was then that she discovered that she held in it an old silver goblet!

A JINX!

It was something of a surprise on answering my doorbell one morning to find a gipsy woman standing there, basketful of pegs and brightly coloured items hanging on her arm.

Usually my St. Bernard dog, though basically a very gentle and docile animal would warn me of any stranger who approached, and often her very size would intimidate any unwanted 'guests' so that they moved no further to the house than the outer gate. Today, however, I was surprised to look past the gipsy and see Schnorbitz sitting in the corner of the garden perfectly still just looking at the intruder. This fact gave me the first sensation of something out of the ordinary. Had this travelling woman some power over animals that produced what was apparently a semi-hypnotic state in the dog?

I'm afraid my husband and I have always been rather too over protective with our pets, and the thought that this unkempt woman standing there had in some way hurt our precious Snorby made me more sharp with her than perhaps I normally would have been. With scarcely a glance at her wares I pointed quite dramatically I suppose to the exit, "Take that rubbish away with you!" I rapped out.

She moved slowly, unwillingly away, and as she reached the gate she turned and uttered a warning, "Bad luck will come ere midnight, you mark my words!" and with that she disappeared down the road.

Telling myself that I didn't believe a word of it and patting Snorby to reassure me that she had not suffered in any way I

52

carried on with my normal household duties of 'vaccing', dusting, and preparing the lunch.

My husband was due home for the meal at one o'clock, so after setting the timer on the oven and preparing the table I sank back thankfully to await his arrival. Being undisturbed I suppose I must have dozed, for wakening with a start I looked at the clock and was horrified to find that it showed three o'clock!

Jumping up I ran to the window — where was John? He was never late! What had happened? The gipsy's curse leapt to my mind, and though trying to tell myself that it was nonsense to think that way the uneasy feeling stayed with me.

I reached for the phone intending to ring the office but as I did so the outer door opened and in walked John.

"What has happened? Where have you been? I've been worried sick," I gasped.

He looked at me in amazement as he said "What on earth is the matter? It's only one o'clock and I'm on time."

Looking at the clock I could scarcely believe my eyes when it showed clearly that it was only just after one and not three. Opening the oven door it was obvious that the lunch was ready exactly as planned.

I spent the rest of the day on tenterhooks — keeping one eye on the dog and the other, wary and watchful on the clock for John's return at tea-time, but all went on as normal.

Nevertheless it was with much relief that I heard the church clock strike midnight, and with it the sense of uncertainty passed.

What had caused that two hour lapse in time? I'm sure I was not asleep for so long. Do you think that travelling Romany had caused some trance like state — a trip into 'no man's land' to punish me by creating terror that something unknown had happened to John?

Snorby has just come and pushed her wet nose into my hand. She seems to be saying, "Forget it. It happened to me too you know."

My dear St. Bernard was right. The story I am recording happened over a year ago, and we have lived happily and contentedly since. One thing is sure though. I shall remember next time we have such a traveller at the door, that a few pence for a handful of clothes pegs is a small price to pay for one's peace of mind.

DREAMS

What a strange part of our make-up is the subconscious! I don't know whether you have ever found a satisfactory explanation for your dreams that really makes sense. Perhaps you have. I feel I have not (this with all apologies to those experts who have made a study of the subject, and who will certainly have gone into it much more deeply than I have been able to do).

Various theories have been put forward — some plainly ridiculous, like the suggestion that cheese at supper-time has a profound influence on our dream pattern. I find Dr Freud's ideas believable in some instances, for example when he writes that many of our dreams spring from emotions that we suppress subconsciously or sometimes even consciously when we are awake, but in sleep they come out and often reveal unfulfilled desires and also fears. *All* my dreams though, I cannot place in that category, though admittedly *some* could.

I know the sleeping position of the body effects the sleep pattern, and that if I lie on my back in bed my dreams are frightening and nightmarish, lying on the left side they are made up of unrelated snatches and snippets fusing into a semi-reasonable sequence of events.

Sometimes we must admit that our dreams are present in such very light sleep and are so near the surface of consciousness that they join up with reality as *may* have happened in the following instance:

My husband and I had settled down for the night. He was

soon obviously 'soundly' asleep, but as frequently happens in my case it was quite a time before I dozed off, lying on my right side as usual to avoid dreaming. This time I was not able to do so for it must have been a full half-hour before my subconscious mind evoked a very vivid dream. It was quite clear — no disconnected snippets. In it I was standing at the kitchen window making a cup of tea when I heard a scratching noise on the pane. Ignoring it, as it has always been our principle never to answer the door or go outside after dark, I carried the cup of tea to the table and sat quietly drinking. The noise at the window grew louder, the scratching became a tapping and the tapping turned to a banging and the banging became a crash at which I awakened with a start. What a relief to find that I had been dreaming, and I was soon fast asleep again.

The next morning on going into the kitchen I was horrified to find glass all over the floor and the window quite badly broken. Not only that but — there on the table was the remains of a cup of tea!

I never did find out how that window was broken and who had made that cup of tea. My husband denies all knowledge of the affair though naturally he is as anxious as I am to find out who was responsible.

Do *you* think that I was the culprit?